To librarians, who open their doors to
the world every day —L. A.

To all the friends who made me feel so
welcome when I moved to the U.S.
Thank you! —J. C.

Farrar Straus Giroux Books for Young Readers
An imprint of Macmillan Publishing Group, LLC
120 Broadway, New York, NY 10271

Text copyright © 2020 by Linda Ashman
Illustrations copyright © 2020 by Joey Chou
All rights reserved
Color separations by Bright Arts (H.K.) Ltd.
Printed in China by Toppan Leefung Printing Ltd.,
Dongguan City, Guangdong Province
Designed by Aurora Parlagreco
First edition, 2020
10 9 8 7 6 5 4 3 2 1

mackids.com

Library of Congress Cataloging-in-Publication Data is
available.
ISBN 978-0-374-31318-0

Our books may be purchased in bulk for promotional,
educational, or business use. Please contact your local
bookseller or the Macmillan Corporate and Premium
Sales Department at (800) 221-7945 ext. 5442 or by email
at MacmillanSpecialMarkets@macmillan.com.

WAYS TO WELCOME

Linda Ashman
pictures by **Joey Chou**

FARRAR STRAUS GIROUX
NEW YORK

aves and shakes
And warm hellos—
Eye to eye
And nose to nose.

Soothing words.
An expert guide—

Step by step
And side by side.

Cheery classroom.
Friendly grin.

"Good to meet you—
come on in!"

Helping hands.

A rescued hat.

CAFÉ

Cups of tea
And a lively chat.

A work of art.
A small bouquet.

An invitation—

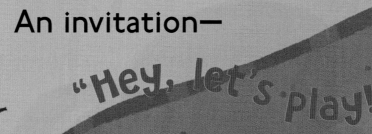
"Hey, let's play!"

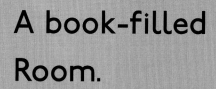

A book-filled
Room.

A song, a rhyme.

A sniff.
A pat.

A gentle hug.
A comfy bed that's
Safe and snug.

ARRIVALS

A homemade sign.
Excited cheers.

WELCOME HOME

Welcome

GRANDPA
&
GRANDMA

A special gift
And happy tears.

BlOOMS to buzz.

A splashy bath.
Starter homes on a
Shady path.

Shelter from the rain and heat.

Garden treasures—
Tart and sweet.

An offering,
A smiling face

That lights an unfamiliar place.

A welcome can be warm
Or cold,

Shy and quiet,

Big and bold.

Meant for someone new
And small—

Or not so new
And very tall.

It sends a message loud and clear:

Hello, friend.
I'm glad you're here.